The Littlest
Lighthouse
Keeper

A catalogue record for this book is available from the British Library.

ISBN 978 1 84538 958 1

Author Heidi Howarth
Illustrator Daniel Howarth
Editor Clare Weaver
Designer Alix Wood
Consultant Anne Faundez

Publisher Steve Evans
Creative Director Zeta Davies

Printed and bound in China

The Littlest
Lighthouse
Keeper

Heidi Howarth
Illustrated by Daniel Howarth

QED Publishing

QED

Henry loved to be by the sea.
He loved the smell and the
sound of the ocean.

He lived in a lighthouse
by the bay and helped the
old lighthouse keeper.

Henry squeezed through the tiniest gaps and reached the highest cogs. The lighthouse ran like clockwork. In return for all his hard work, Henry's tummy was always full and his nest was really cosy.

Today, Henry had been busy at work all morning when he noticed something. The lighthouse was quiet. The only sound was the tick tock of the old keeper's clock.

Henry scampered downstairs.

The lighthouse keeper had gone.
All he had left was a note saying
"Gone to the dentist!"

But he had
forgotten one very
important thing.
Henry could
not read.

Henry climbed sadly back to his nest.
Tap … Tap … Tap!
A puffin was tapping on the glass.

"Are you hungry?" she asked.
"I wasn't sure if you ate fish like
me, so I brought you this."

Henry pushed open the window.
What a feast – berries, nuts and seeds.

"Oh, thank you," said Henry.
"This is perfect. I was so hungry."

With a full tummy
and a new friend,
Henry returned
to his chores.

There was one job Henry had never tried on his own. He had always sat safe in the keeper's pocket as the old man climbed the steep ladder to the top of the lighthouse.

"I can do this," Henry said to himself.

Looking up, it all
seemed so scary.
Henry's paws
were trembling ...
they slipped and
Arrrrrh!
Henry fell.

Henry's eyes were tightly shut ... he was scared to open them. He felt he was floating. "Hello," said a gentle voice. Henry slowly opened one eye. There was a spider, glossy black with big bead-like eyes.

"My web caught you," she said.
"Where were you going?"

"To the lamp at the top of the lighthouse,"
Henry replied. "I need to check it is working."
"I will climb with you," said Spider.

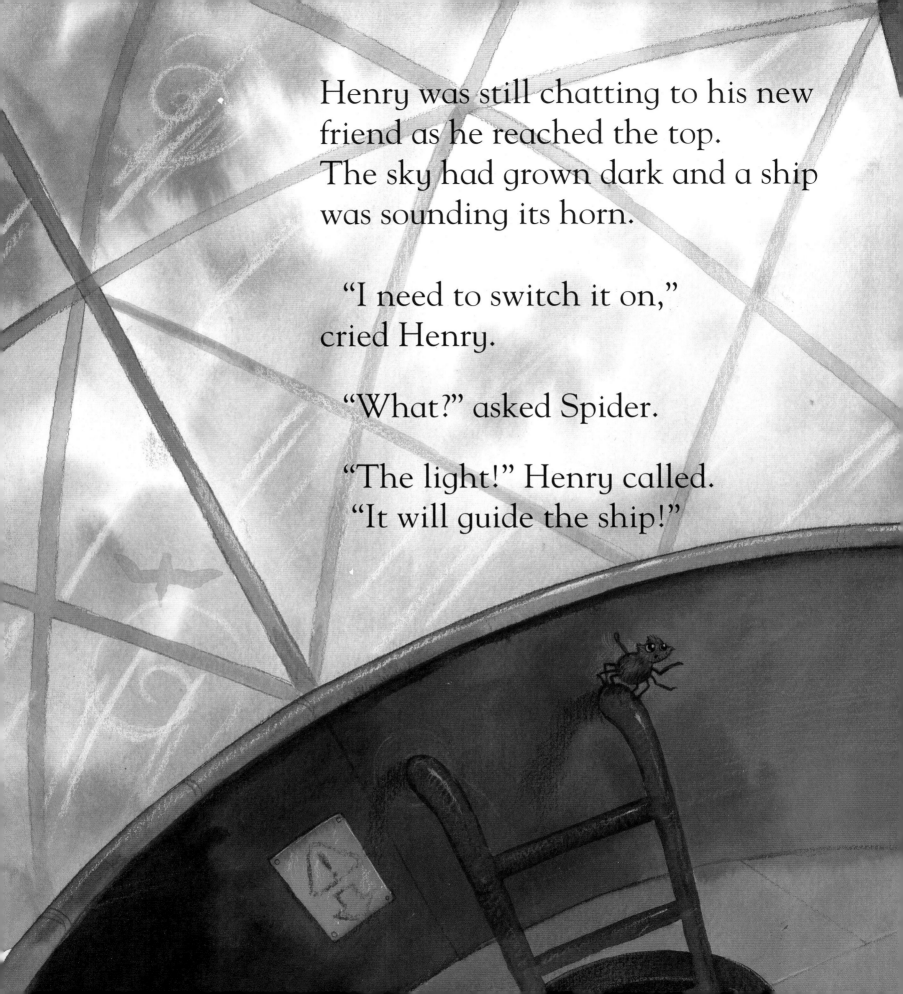

Henry was still chatting to his new
friend as he reached the top.
The sky had grown dark and a ship
was sounding its horn.

"I need to switch it on,"
cried Henry.

"What?" asked Spider.

"The light!" Henry called.
"It will guide the ship!"

Henry pulled and pulled as
hard as he could … CLICK!

Nothing happened.
The lighthouse was still dark.
Henry turned the switch off.

Henry knew there was a spare bulb, but it was right at the bottom of the lighthouse and he was at the top. There was no time to fetch it.

Spider seemed to have gone and with no lighthouse keeper to help what could Henry do?

Suddenly, Henry heard a sound.
Puffin fluttered above him, with
Spider dangling from a silvery strand.

"Come on," said Spider, "I have
a plan that might just work and
I have brought some help."

The plan was simple. Henry and Spider climbed onto Puffin's back and down she flew. Spider span a web and they put the spare bulb safely in it.

Quickly, they hopped back onto Puffin and off she flew to the top of the lighthouse.

Spider and Henry hopped to the floor. Henry took out the old bulb and screwed the new bulb into place.

What had seemed impossible for Henry on his own had been easy for the three friends working together. They smiled.

Henry pulled the switch.
A bright beam of light
shone out across the bay.

"We did it!" cried Henry.

The friends cheered as they watched the ship sail safely away from the sharp rocks below.

Henry was so tired he did not know he had fallen asleep until his nose twitched with a delicious smell… Sizzling bacon!

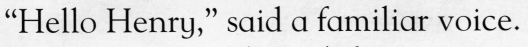

"Hello Henry," said a familiar voice.
"I am so sorry to have left you."

"What a wonderful job you have done," he
said. "You may be the littlest lighthouse keeper
but you make a really
big difference."

He gave Henry a special little lighthouse keeper's cap, and he didn't forget Henry's new friends either.

Spider could spin her webs wherever she wanted and Puffin had fresh fish to eat every day.

But best of all they all had each other.

Notes for Parents and Teachers

- Look at the front cover of the book together. Talk about the picture. Can the children guess what the story is about? Read the title together.

- When the children first read the story (or had it read to them) how did they think the story was going to end? Were they right? Discuss other ideas of how the story might have ended.

- Ask the children to take it in turns to try to read the story aloud. Help them with any difficult words and remember to praise the children for their efforts in reading the book.

- Henry may be very small but he is also very useful for jobs that the old lighthouse keeper is just too big to do. Talk to the children about animals that also have real-life jobs, or used to in the past. For example, police dogs and horses, or pigeons that were used to carry messages. What other animals can the children think of and what jobs do they imagine they would be good at?

- This story lends itself to group artwork. Help the children to design and build their own lighthouse. Discuss what features a lighthouse needs. Where would it need to be located? It needs to be easily seen. It needs to have a light. What colours do the children think it should be? Should it be really bright to stand out?

- Being a lighthouse keeper is a very unusual job. Have the children heard of a lighthouse keeper? Discuss with them what jobs a lighthouse keeper has to do each day. Would they like to be a lighthouse keeper?

- A lighthouse keeper is there for the safety of others. Get the children to make a list of other jobs like this that people may do.

- Ask the children what their favourite job would be. Which job is the most popular? Is it the same for boys and girls?

- Henry, Spider and Puffin discover that working together as a team gets the job done. Can the children think of any other examples when working together gets something done more easily than working alone? Have the children ever worked as part of a team?